SHY CHARLES

ROSEMARY WELLS

SCHOLASTIC INC.
New York   Toronto   London   Auckland   Sydney
Mexico City   New Delhi   Hong Kong

ISBN 0-439-13986-4

Copyright © 1988 by Rosemary Wells.
All rights reserved.
Published by Scholastic Inc., 555 Broadway, New York, NY 10012,
by arrangement with Dial Books for Young Readers, a division of Penguin Putnam Inc.
SCHOLASTIC and associated logos are trademarks
and/or registered trademarks of Scholastic Inc.

12 11 10 9 8 7 6 5 4 3 2   0 1 2 3 4/0

Printed in the U.S.A.   14

Designed by Jane Byers Bierhorst
The art for each picture consists of a black ink and watercolor painting,
which is camera-separated and reproduced in full color.

For shy Victoria

Charles was happy as he could be,

But he liked to play alone.
He wouldn't talk to Wanda Sue,

And he never went near the phone.

"It's a new day," said Charles's mother.
"Let's go in the store and say hello.
We'll buy a sweet-potato pie.
And we'll say good-bye before we go."

"Wonderful morning!" said Mrs. Belinski.
"A chocolate surprise for my beautiful boy!"

"Say thank you," whispered Charles's mother.
"Thank you!" yelled Mrs. Belinski. "Enjoy!"

His mother told him, "Say good-bye!"
Charles hid inside a flour sack.
"Good-bye with kisses," said Mrs. Belinski.
"Someday when he's big, he'll kiss me back!"

"I'm so embarrassed," said Charles's mother.
"You never say good-bye or thank you.
  Lucky for you that I'm so nice.
  Another mother would spank you!"

"This can't go on," said Charles's dad.
"I'm sick and tired of thank-you fights.
   It's time he played football or joined the ballet."

Next Tuesday Charles was in tights.

"Isn't he sweet!" cried Madame La Fleur.
Charles wouldn't say maybe or no or yes.

For a week he pretended to be asleep.

Charles was not a success.

So Charles's father took him to town
And bought him some beautiful football things.
The shirt was scarlet with shoulder pads.
The helmet had silver wings.

"Charles," said his father, "you'll be the best!
Like lightning you'll streak across the grass.
Like butter you'll melt the defensive line.
And you'll throw the winning pass!"

Charles trembled like an autumn leaf.
"Hi!" roared the coach, "my name is Fred.

"He doesn't look so well to me.
Take him home and put him to bed."

"Charles!" said his dad. "You're a jelly roll!
You're just a cowardly custard.
You're like a sandwich without the bread
Not to mention the ham and mustard.
How will you ever go to school
or find a job or get married?"
Charles sat down and cried so hard...

He had to be carried.

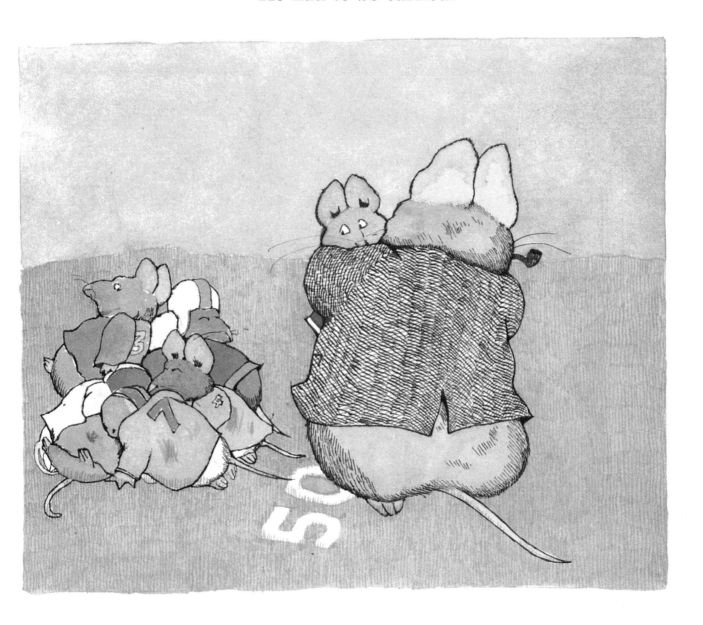

Then Charles's father murmured low,
"A baby-sitter is coming tonight.
You know the one. It's Mrs. Block.
And everything will be all right."

The sun went down. The sitter came.
His parents left at six o'clock.

Charles skedaddled up the stairs.
"Come back, little pushcake!" cried Mrs. Block.

Charles played happily in his room.
He made a spaceship out of his chairs.
Suddenly there was a terrible crash....

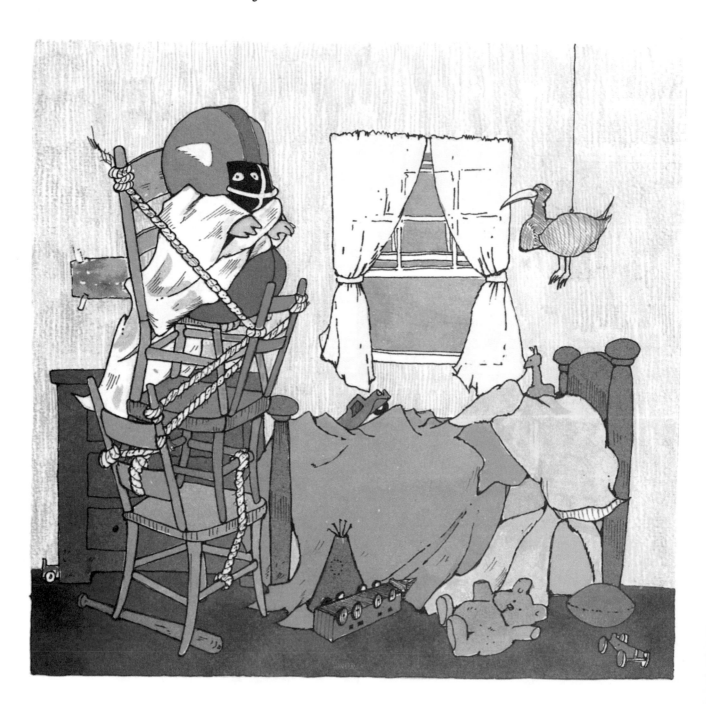

Mrs. Block had fallen downstairs.

Charles got her onto the sofa.
He told her, "Now, don't be nervous!"

He brought her a blanket and cocoa,
Then he called the emergency service.

"He saved my life," moaned Mrs. Block.
"He's a prince, a gem, a hero!"

And everyone shouted, "Thank you, Charles!"
But Charles said…

Zero.